Who Took the Farmer's Hat?

WhoTookThe

HarperCollins*Publishers*

Farmer's ?

story by Joan L. Nodset • pictures by Fritz Siebel

For Lila R. Mitchell

Who Took the Farmer's Hat?
Text copyright © 1963 by Joan L. Nodset
Illustrations copyright © 1963 by Fritz Siebel
All rights reserved. Manufactured in China.
No part of this book may be used or reproduced
in any manner whatsoever without written permission
except in the case of brief quotations embodied
in critical articles and reviews.
For information address HarperCollins Children's Books,
a division of HarperCollins Publishers,
10 East 53rd Street, New York, NY 10022.

Library of Congress Catalog Card Number: 62-17964
ISBN 0-06-024565-4
ISBN 0-06-024566-2 (lib. bdg.)
ISBN 0-06-443174-6 (pbk.)
First Harper Trophy edition, 1988

The farmer had a hat, an old brown hat.

Oh, how he liked that old brown hat!

But the wind took it, and away it went.

The farmer ran fast, but the wind went faster.

So the farmer had to look for it.

He looked and he looked

and he looked. No old brown hat.

He saw Squirrel. "Squirrel, did you see
my old brown hat?" said the farmer.

"No," said Squirrel.
"I saw a fat round brown bird
in the sky.
A bird with no wings."

The farmer saw Mouse. "Mouse, did you see my old brown hat?" said the farmer.

"No," said Mouse.
"I saw a big round brown mousehole
in the grass.
I ran to it, but away it went."

The farmer saw Fly.
"Fly, did you see
my old brown hat?"
said the farmer.

"No," said Fly.
"I saw a flat round brown hill.
The hill was in a tree.
And then that hill took off,
and away it went."

The farmer saw Goat.
"Goat, did you see
my old brown hat?"
said the farmer.

"No," said Goat.

"I saw a funny round brown flowerpot.

I was going to eat it,

but the wind took that flowerpot away."

The farmer saw Duck. "Duck, did you see
my old brown hat?" said the farmer.

"No," said Duck.

"I saw a silly round brown boat,
but Bird took that."

The farmer saw Bird.
"Bird, did you take
my old brown hat?"
said the farmer.

"No," said Bird.

"I saw this nice round brown nest,
but no hat."

The farmer looked
at the nest in the tree.
A nice old round brown nest.

Bird was in it.

And an egg was in it.

"Oh, my!" said the farmer.

"Like it?" said Bird.

"I like it," said the farmer.

"Oh, yes, I like that nice round brown nest.

It looks a *little* like my old brown hat.

But I see it is a nice round brown nest."

The farmer has a new brown hat.

Oh, how he likes that new brown hat!

And how Bird likes that old brown nest!